The Adventures of the Prickly Pear and the Happy Hoglet

Beginning the Journey of the Mental Ninja

Written By

Edward P. Buchanan, MD

Illustrated By

Matthew A. Buchanan

ISBN: 978-1-4834-0599-5 (sc)
ISBN: 978-1-4834-0600-8 (e)

Lulu Publishing Services rev. date: 12/26/2013

Dedication

To James and Carole Buchanan,
Your constant and unconditional love have made possible this story
and its images. Thank you for giving so much to your children.

What is a Mental Ninja?

Prickly and Happy have begun their journey on the path to becoming Mental Ninjas. Being able to control your feelings in the face of life's many obstacles, no matter how big or small, is a characteristic which will serve for a lifetime. The journey to achieving this status is long and requires constant work and evaluation, but the rewards are enduring. Learn with our friends as they discover and implement one of life's most powerful tools.

Once upon a time, there lived a particularly Prickly Pear and his friend, the Happy Hoglet.

They were best friends. They did everything together. They went to the same school and had the same friends.

One day, at the bus stop, Smelly DurianFruit started to bully the younger kids.

He said, "Prickly, your spines are too long. Happy, you are too hairy!"

Prickly thought, "Are my spines too long, do I look funny?" Prickly felt sad.

Happy wondered, "Why does Smelly always look angry? Why does he never smile?"

Once they got on the bus, they could not sit together. They both sat with someone new.

Prickly sat next to Dani Dish-Cleaner. He did not smile or say hello to Dani. Prickly was lonely because he couldn't sit with his friend Happy.

Happy sat next to Terry Toenail Clipper and learned that they liked the same slam ball team and they were going to the same wilderness scout camp. Happy made a new friend.

At school, their teacher, Miss Chalk-Eraser, returned their
math tests. Both Prickly Pear and Happy Hoglet earned the same
grade, a B+.

Prickly was discouraged. He thought, "I am just not smart enough to get A's."

Happy knew that he could do better. He thought, "I will study more after school."

At recess, Prickly and Happy wanted to play blaster ball. They were not picked to be on any team.

Prickly was gloomy. He thought, "If I was better, I would have been picked."

Happy played with Owen Octopus. He had so much fun that he did not even think about blaster ball.

Prickly Pear and Happy Hoglet were on the same baseball team, the Northland Ninjas. The Ninjas won the game, even with the Happy Hoglet and the Prickly Pear striking out 2 times.

Prickly cried, "I am just not a good baseball player."

Happy thought, "I will practice for the next game and do better for my team."

After the game, Gary Grasshopper invited some of his teammates to his house to have some pizza and ice cream. Happy and Prickly were not invited.

Prickly Pear was sad. He
started to cry. "No one likes me!"

Happy was also
disappointed. But, he knew
that he would have fun
walking home with his
best friend, Prickly.

During their walk home from the game, Happy saw that his friend had been crying. "What is the matter, Prickly?"

Prickly told Happy about all of the miserable things that had happened that day.

Happy said, "Wow, Prickly, the same things happened to me!"

Prickly said, "Then why are you not crying?"

Happy said, "When things don't turn out exactly the way I want, I try to look at it a different way. When I do this, I always find something good, which makes me happy."

Prickly did not know if he could do this, 'look at it a different way.'

Happy said, "I have been doing this since I was a little hoglet. I just don't like feeling sad, so I try to always find something good, no matter what happens.

Prickly, You should practice feeling happy and then you will be."

Suddenly, a huge truck drove by and splashed mud all over them. Prickly began to get upset. Slowly he thought about what his friend had told him . . . 'Look at it a different way.'

Happy knew that his friend was thinking very hard, and was afraid that he would be unhappy again.

"How do you feel right now, Prickly?"

Prickly yelled out gleefully, " I feel great, do you know why?" And before Happy could answer, he squealed, "Because now we have a reason to go swimming!"

They rushed home, changed into their swim suits, and jumped into the pool. Prickly was happy because he had learned an important lesson. Happy was happy because he helped his friend. They had big, joyful smiles on their faces as they splashed in the pool.

The End.

After working for over 10 years at Children's Hospitals across the country, the author has helped treat many different ailments. What he has observed during this time, is that no matter how difficult the issue, the most powerful treatment is a positive mental attitude. This tale is intended to teach and reinforce the importance of that mantra, to provide both young and old with the tools to deal with life's difficult times. While this is not a novel idea, introducing this concept early to children will help them understand the importance of positive mental imagery and allow them to begin to develop these empowering mental pathways.

Lightning Source UK Ltd.
Milton Keynes UK
UKIC03n1845271015
261506UK00004B/10